For Betty, who sorts everybody out (especially Little Lenny!) ~ S S

For Matt Upsher, his family, his friends and all those he inspired ~ C P

Copyright © 2011 by Good Books, Intercourse, PA 17534
International Standard Book Number: 978-1-56148-725-7

Text copyright © Steve Smallman 2011
Illustrations copyright © Caroline Pedler 2011
Original edition published in English by Little Tiger Press,
an imprint of Magi Publications, London, England, 2011
LTP/1400/0222/0311 • Printed in China

Cataloging-in-Publication Data is available from
the Good Books website.

Who's Afraid of the Big Bad Bunny?

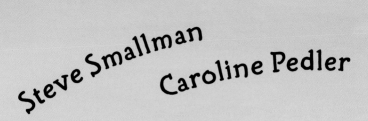

Steve Smallman   Caroline Pedler

Good Books

Intercourse, PA 17534, 800/762-7171,
www.GoodBooks.com

"I'm hungry!" said Little Lenny Bunny.

"I'm **very** hungry!" said Slightly Bigger Benny Bunny.

"I'm **very**, **very** hungry!"
said Much Bigger Barney Bunny.

"Well, someone had better go to
the garden and get some carrots
because there are none left!"
said Itty Bitty Betty Bunny.

"I'll go!" said Little Lenny. And off he went.

Little Lenny Bunny had just pulled up
one big, juicy carrot when
out jumped ...

a
Big
Bad
Bully
Bunny!

He **pushed** poor Lenny on to his little bunny bottom and **snatched** the carrot.

"You can't have this carrot!" he shouted.

"Why not?" squeaked Little Lenny.

"Because you're really, really stupid!" bellowed the Big Bad Bully Bunny.

"And if you tell anyone that I took your carrot, I'll squash you flat!"

Poor Lenny Bunny went back to his burrow empty-handed.

"Why didn't you bring us any carrots?" asked his brothers and sister.

"Because I'm too stupid," said Little Lenny in a very small voice.

"No, you're not! Who told you that?" they asked.

But Little Lenny Bunny
wouldn't tell.

"Don't worry!" said Slightly
Bigger Benny Bunny. "I'll get
us some carrots!"
And off he went.

Benny Bunny had just pulled up
two juicy-looking carrots
when . . .
out jumped the **Big Bad Bully Bunny.**

He **pushed** over poor Benny Bunny and **snatched** the carrots.

"You can't have these carrots!"

he shouted.

"Why not?"
gasped Benny Bunny.

"Because you're really, really **ugly!**

And if you tell anyone that I took your carrots, **I'll squash you flat!**"

Poor Benny Bunny went back home empty-handed.

"Why didn't **you** bring us any carrots?" asked Barney and Betty.

"Because I'm too ugly," said Benny Bunny in a very small voice.

"No, you're not! Who told you that?" they asked.

But Benny Bunny wouldn't tell.

"Don't worry!" said Much Bigger Barney Bunny. "I'll get us some carrots!"

And off he went.

Barney Bunny had just
pulled up three juicy-looking
carrots when . . .

out jumped the
**Big
Bad
Bully
Bunny.**

"You can't have these carrots!" he shouted.

"W... w... why not?" stuttered Barney Bunny.

"Because you're really, really **fat** and **wobbly!** And if you tell anyone that I took your carrots, I'll squash you **flat!**"

Poor Barney Bunny went back home empty-handed.

"Why didn't **you** bring us any carrots **either**?" cried Betty.

"Because I'm too fat and wobbly," sniffed Barney Bunny in a very small voice.

"No, you're not! Who told you that?" she asked.

But Barney Bunny wouldn't tell.

"This is just silly!" shouted Itty Bitty Betty Bunny.

"Barney, you are **not** fat or wobbly!

Benny, you're **not** ugly!

And you are **not** stupid, Lenny."

"Now. Who's been saying these nasty things to you?"

"The Big Bad Bully Bunny," said Lenny, Benny and Barney Bunny in three very small voices.

"Well, why didn't you say something?" said Betty. "Together we can best any bad bully!"

Itty Bitty Betty Bunny took all of her brothers to the garden to pick some carrots. Lenny, Benny and Barney Bunny were very nervous but they quickly pulled up...

a
great
big
pile of
carrots.

Out jumped...

... the Big Bad **Bully** Bunny.

"You can't have those carrots!"

he shouted.

"Why not?"

asked Betty Bunny.

"Because you're just a stupid, ugly, big, fat, wobbly girl!"

bellowed the Big Bad Bully Bunny.

"No, I'm not,"
said the little rabbit.
"**You** are!"

"**N**...no, I'm not!"
cried the Big Bad Bully Bunny.
"Just give me
these carrots...
now!"

Then Betty, Lenny, Benny and Barney
Bunny all shouted

"NO!"

The Big Bad Bully Bunny was so

surprised that he fell on to his big,

bully bunny bottom

with a great big bump.

"But I'm hungry!" wailed the Bad Bully Bunny, who suddenly didn't feel so big any more. "Give me some carrots!" he whined. "Now!"

Betty whispered something to Lenny, Benny, and Barney. And they all heaved and pushed until they tipped over the wheelbarrow full of carrots . . .

...and nearly squashed him

flat!

And he never **ever** bullied
bunnies again.